Santa Claus Doesn't Mop Floors

**Read more books
by Debbie Dadey
and Marcia Thornton Jones!**

Ghostville
Elementary®

Santa Claus Doesn't Mop Floors

by

Debbie Dadey and Marcia Thornton Jones

illustrated by John Steven Gurney

A
LITTLE APPLE
PAPERBACK

SCHOLASTIC INC.

New York Toronto London Auckland Sydney
Mexico City New Delhi Hong Kong Buenos Aires

Santa Claus Doesn't Mop Floors, ISBN 0-590-44477-8
Text copyright © 1991 by Debra S. Dadey and Marcia Thornton Jones.
Illustrations copyright © 1991 by Scholastic Inc.

Mrs. Claus Doesn't Climb Telephone Poles, ISBN 0-439-40832-6
Text copyright © 2002 by Debra S. Dadey and Marcia Thornton Jones.
Illustrations copyright © 2002 by Scholastic Inc.

12 11 10 9 8 7 6 5 4 3 2 1   3 4 5 6 7 8/0

Printed in the U.S.A.   40

First compilation printing, December 2003

*To Allison, Jared, and Nathan —
and to Santa Claus!*

Contents

1 A Sticky Situation   1

2 Mr. Jolly   8

3 A Peculiar Helper   13

4 A Chill in the Air   19

5 A Jolly Disaster   29

6 Checking It Twice   35

7 Let It Snow!   41

8 Magic?   48

9 Ho! Ho! Ho!   55

10 You Better Watch Out   61

11 Santa's Challenge   66

12 Santa's Miracle   69

1

A Sticky Situation

"That's it!" Mr. Dobson, the janitor, screamed at the third-grade classroom. "I've had enough of your shenanigans."

Mrs. Ewing stared at Mr. Dobson from her desk. It was obvious she wasn't used to having an hysterical janitor at her door. She had only been the third-grade substitute teacher for one week, and she was already showing signs of battle fatigue. "Calm down, Mr. Dobson," she said. "Tell me what's wrong."

"I'll tell you what's wrong," he snapped. "Somebody took peanut butter from the food drive box and spread it all over the stair railing!" He held out his hands as proof. Sure enough, they were covered with brown sticky peanut butter.

1

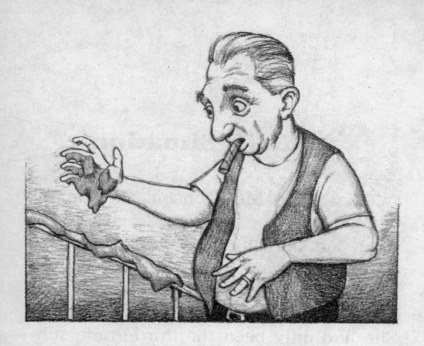

"It looks like he's been making mud pies," Eddie giggled.

Mr. Dobson silenced him with a glare. "It was somebody in this class, wasn't it?"

Mrs. Ewing stood up. "Mr. Dobson, I'm sorry about the peanut butter, but I don't think you can blame anybody without proof."

Mr. Dobson looked like he was ready to explode. There wasn't a sound from

2

the kids as he hissed, "I have cleaned up vomit. I've mopped up sour milk from the floor. I have even scraped bubble gum from the ceilings in the bathroom. But this time it has gone too far. I will not clean up another mess made by these brats. I quit!"

"But you can't," Mrs. Ewing interrupted. "Christmas will be here in just a few weeks. How will you buy presents? Who will help clean up after the holiday parties?"

Mr. Dobson smiled like a lunatic. "My present will be to see these urchins clean up after themselves. And they can start with the stairs!" With that, he left.

Mrs. Ewing faced the third-grade class. Her red-painted lips were pressed in a thin line and a wrinkle messed up her forehead. She ran her fingers through her short curly hair and took a deep breath. "I can't believe anyone in this class would be so thoughtless, so cruel!" she said. "Mr. Dobson has worked hard to keep this building clean, and you repay him with a prank like that!"

Melody raised her hand. "But maybe it wasn't anyone in our class."

"Maybe not," Mrs. Ewing sighed. "I'd hate to think anyone in this room would take the food we've been collecting for the poor. But you do have a reputation for causing trouble."

Nobody could argue with her about that. They hadn't had recess for a month before Halloween. That's when each kid had brought in a spider to set loose in the principal's office. And then their teacher quit after she found her desk drawers full of shaving cream. Of course, everything changed after their new teacher, Mrs. Jeepers, came.

There was something about Mrs. Jeepers that made them straighten up fast.

4

Her eyes would flash at the first sign of trouble, and the green brooch she always wore would start to glow. Some kids thought she was some kind of monster or vampire. Before Mrs. Jeepers left for a Christmas vacation in Romania, she made the children promise to be nice to the substitute teacher. Unfortunately, Mrs. Jeepers forgot about Mr. Dobson.

Howie spoke up. "Mr. Dobson isn't really going to quit, is he? After all, he's threatened to leave before!"

Mrs. Ewing shook her head. "This time, I think he's serious."

"But who will clean the building?" Eddie asked.

Principal Davis interrupted from the door. "You will clean the building," he snapped. "Mr. Dobson has just quit his job, thanks to you."

Eddie sat up straight. "You can't prove it was us!"

5

"Oh, no?" Principal Davis stomped over to the trash can. Every kid in the room held his or her breath as the principal stooped down and pulled out two empty peanut butter jars. "How do you explain these?"

Eddie jabbed Howie in the back. "You moron," he sputtered. "You should have dumped those in another class!"

But it was too late now.

"Until I find a replacement for Mr. Dobson," Principal Davis said through clenched teeth, "this class is in charge of cleaning. And you can start with the stair railing!"

2

Mr. Jolly

"I wonder when Principal Davis is going to hire a new janitor?" Liza asked as she pushed blonde hair out of her eyes.

Eddie slapped the mop around on the hall floor. "It's been a whole week since Mr. Dobson quit. I'm sick of emptying trash and mopping the floors every recess."

"We wouldn't be doing it at all if you hadn't come up with that peanut butter idea," Howie snapped.

"It was only peanut butter!" Eddie sputtered.

Melody tugged on her black braid. "It really wasn't a nice thing to do. And now poor Mr. Dobson is without a job during Christmas!"

"It was his choice!" Eddie's face was

turning as red as his hair. "He didn't have to quit. Besides, who cares about Christmas anyway!"

Liza, Howie, and Melody looked at each other. Ever since Eddie's mother had died, his father refused to celebrate Christmas.

"Everybody likes Christmas," Liza said softly.

"Not me!" Eddie announced. "Christmas is for sissies."

"Sissies!" boomed a deep voice behind them.

All four kids turned to see Principal Davis and a very fat man standing in the hall.

"I'd like to introduce Mr. Jolly," Principal Davis said. "He's our new janitor."

Mr. Jolly smiled at them. His blue eyes twinkled under his bushy white eyebrows, and a smile could barely be seen from under his thick white beard and

9

mustache. A thin curl of smoke circled above the pipe he puffed on. He could've passed for somebody's grandfather if it hadn't been for his clothes. Most grand-fathers don't wear hot pink T-shirts with green-and-pink slacks. He even had on bright green tennis shoes to match.

Melody broke the silence. "We sure are glad to meet you."

"I bet you are," Mr. Jolly chuckled as he took the mop from Eddie. "Now you kids can go out to recess, and I'll clean up this mess," he said as he pulled his beard. And with that he began mopping the floor. The keys hanging from his green belt jingled as he worked. The floor seemed to sparkle wherever he mopped.

"Boy, he sure works fast," Liza com-mented.

"Who cares?" Eddie said. "Let's get outside."

Once they were on the playground, the four ex-janitors gathered under the oak tree. Their breaths looked like Mr. Jolly's pipe smoke as they talked.

"Mr. Jolly sure seems nice," Liza said.

"But he's awfully fat," Howie pointed out.

Melody rolled her eyes. "Big deal, so he's fat. I'm just glad we don't have to mop the floor anymore."

Howie wanted to be a doctor, and he was always talking about health. "Being fat is bad for you."

"So's this, ice breath," Eddie said with a laugh. And then he smacked Howie right in the face with a snowball.

After that, it was all-out war. The four kids were so busy throwing snowballs, they didn't see that Mr. Jolly was watching them from the window, and that he was writing things down in a little red notebook.

3

A Peculiar Helper

Nobody gave Mr. Jolly a second thought. At least, not until the end of that week. They were all sitting at the lunch table, slurping down chicken noodle soup.

"Who is that?" Melody asked with wide eyes.

Howie, Eddie, and Liza glanced across the room.

"It's Mr. Jolly," Liza said, as if she had just solved a hard math problem.

"I know that," Melody snapped. "But who's that with him?"

"I don't see anybody," Howie said.

Eddie shook his head. "I think Melody has gone nuts!"

"I have not," Melody hissed. "You just can't see him."

"I told you she's gone bananas," Eddie

13

said confidently. "Now she's even seeing things."

Melody slammed her spoon on the table. "I'm perfectly fine. You just can't see him because he's behind Mr. Jolly. Look over there now."

They all looked as a very short man walked around Mr. Jolly. He looked just like any school kid, except for his pointy black beard. He was dressed in green from head to toe, and he even wore a little green hat. He waved his arms like he was excited. Mr. Jolly nodded his head every once in a while.

"I've never seen anybody so short," Liza whispered.

"He can't help it if he's short," Howie said smugly.

"I want to know what they're talking about," Eddie said as he stood up. "Let's go find out."

Howie grabbed Eddie. "That's eaves-dropping."

"So?" Eddie shrugged.

"Listening to other people talking isn't very nice," Melody chimed in.

"Who said I'm nice?" Eddie said as he pulled away from Howie. "You'll come, too, if you want to find out who the little man is!"

Liza, Howie, and Melody looked at each other and then followed Eddie. They carried their trays to the trash cans the long way around the cafeteria so they'd have to walk right behind Mr. Jolly and the little man.

"It's a mess, S.C.," the little man was saying. "You'll have to come straighten it out. It's too close to Christmas for you to be fooling around as a janitor. There's real work to be done!"

Mr. Jolly interrupted him. "Eli, this is

15

real work. There's not a thing wrong with being a janitor."

"But we need you at home!"

"You can manage by yourselves, Eli," Mr. Jolly said. "I've got work to do here."

Suddenly Eli cleared his throat and pointed to the four kids with their trays. Howie, Eddie, and Melody looked away as they walked behind Mr. Jolly. But Liza froze.

"We weren't listening," Liza said too loudly. "We were just putting our trays away."

Mr. Jolly tugged on his beard and looked down at her. "You took the long way around, didn't you?" he asked.

Liza looked like she was ready to faint. Instead she barely nodded.

"Well," Mr. Jolly chuckled, "you better go put your tray away, then."

Mr. Jolly glanced down at his friend, Eli. "Like I said, I've got work to do here." Then he pulled out his notebook and began to write in it.

4

A Chill in the Air

"It's freezing in here," Eddie complained. It was the morning after Eli had been in the cafeteria. Eddie, Melody, Liza, and Howie were the first children in their classroom.

"You can see your breath, it's so cold," Howie said. They all took turns blowing cold smoke rings at each other.

"I bet that new janitor forgot to turn on the heat," Liza said.

"What's he trying to do, freeze us to death?" Melody shivered and hugged herself to keep warm.

"We better go find him and tell him to turn up the thermostat," Howie suggested. "Before Principal Davis gets mad and fires him!"

The four kids went to the janitor's room

19

in the basement. Sure enough, there was Mr. Jolly, filling a bucket with sudsy water.

Melody grabbed Howie. "He must be crazy! He's wearing shorts!"

"And a T-shirt," Howie whispered.

The sight of Mr. Jolly's bare legs and arms made Liza shiver. The new janitor still wore his bright green tennis shoes — and no socks!

"Well, good morning," he boomed when he saw the four children. "What can I do for you?"

"We thought we'd remind you to turn on the heat," Howie said. "It's a bit cold here this morning." Little clouds formed as Howie spoke, to prove his point.

"Nonsense!" Mr. Jolly laughed. "It was way too warm in here. I finally had to turn the heat down so I wouldn't melt."

"But it's the dead of winter," Eddie interrupted.

"It's freezing outside," Melody added.

Mr. Jolly peeped out the little window. "Why, there isn't even the tiniest snowflake out there, not a glimmer of ice, nor a spot of slush. It's practically summer today! Now, you kids scoot to class!" With that, Mr. Jolly continued mixing white bubbles into his bucket.

Eddie led his friends down the hall. "I thought this guy was weird," he said. "He's short on brains, as well as having short friends!"

Liza pulled her jacket tight. "I guess we'll just have to make do."

"Not me!" Eddie exclaimed. "I'm getting some heat."

Eddie turned and stomped away, with his friends following. He turned a corner and opened a closet.

"What are you doing?" Howie whispered. "We're not allowed in there."

"We're not allowed to do much of anything," Eddie said as he turned on a light. "But that's never stopped me before." Then he pointed to a big thermostat on the wall. "That's just what we need." Eddie twisted the dial.

"Our worries are over," he said as he shut the closet door. "It ought to be warming up in no time flat."

Eddie was right. In less than twenty minutes they were able to shed their

coats. Some kids even took off their sweaters. They were just settling down to their English work when Melody decided she had to go to the bathroom.

Eddie watched as she left the room, then he raised his hand.

"Yes, Eddie?" Mrs. Ewing asked.

"I need to get something out in the hall," Eddie said. "I need my pencil."

"Well . . . make it quick," Mrs. Ewing snapped.

"Sure thing," Eddie said as he rushed out the door. He spied Melody at the water fountain. She was leaning over, slurping loudly. Eddie sneaked up behind her and dunked her head into the ice-cold water.

Melody stood up, sputtering. "I'm going to get you for that," she said, curling her hand into a fist.

But before she had a chance to

sock him a really good one, Mr. Jolly walked around the corner and ran right into Eddie.

"Gee, Mr. Jolly," Eddie snapped. "You ought to watch where you're going!"

"It serves you right," Melody giggled. Then she glanced up at Mr. Jolly. "Are you okay?"

Mr. Jolly pulled on his beard. A little river of sweat trickled down his nose and then dripped to the floor. He pulled out a green-and-white-checked handkerchief and wiped off his face. "Yes, I think I'll be just fine," he said. "It's just that it's so warm in this blasted building. I can't stand warm temperatures."

"It feels fine to me," Melody said.

"Yeah," Eddie huffed. "It's much warmer than this morning."

Mr. Jolly looked thoughtfully at Eddie, and then he pulled out his little red note-book and jotted something down.

"You're always writing stuff down," Eddie commented. "What is that notebook for, anyway?"

Mr. Jolly dabbed at his forehead. "Oh, it's just a list of some things. But I don't have time to talk now. I have to do something about this temperature." And with a jingling of keys, he was gone.

"Did you hear that?" Eddie groaned. "He'll see that we turned up the thermostat."

But there was nothing Eddie and Melody could do about it because Mrs. Ewing rushed out into the hall and took them each by the arm. "Into the classroom and to your work," she snapped. "This instant!"

They hadn't even finished their English when the temperature started to drop. Mrs. Ewing was the first to notice. She shivered and slipped into her sweater. It wasn't long before all the kids in the class had their sweaters on, too.

Liza rubbed her hands together. "It's so cold, I can hardly write," she whispered.

Howie nodded as he stuck his hands under his armpits. "My hands feel like a frozen fish," he moaned.

During math, Melody started to sniff. "My nose is starting to run."

"I think my pencil is frozen to my hand," Eddie groaned.

By recess time, the kids in Mrs. Ewing's third grade were so cold they didn't even want to go outside. "Nonsense," Mrs. Ewing scolded. "Some fresh air is just what we need. Maybe if we all get some exercise, we'll warm up."

All the kids buttoned up their coats and put on their mittens as they filed outside.

"I don't believe it!" Howie yelled. "It's warmer outside than inside!"

It was true. With the sun shining on them, it felt ten degrees warmer.

"Mr. Jolly's gonna freeze us to death this winter," Melody said. "He told us he hates it warm."

"Maybe we could turn the thermostat back up," Liza suggested.

"No," Howie moaned. "Mr. Jolly would just turn it back to the arctic zone."

"Well, I'm not going to freeze to death all winter long," Eddie snapped.

"What can YOU do?" Melody asked.

Eddie smiled. "I'll make him sorry he ever heard of Bailey Elementary School. He'll be so tired from cleaning up after me, he won't have time to mess with the temperature."

"You can't do that," Liza insisted.

"Why not?" Eddie asked.

"If you do, he'll probably quit his job. And it's almost Christmas. What would Mr. Jolly do without a job during the holidays?" Liza asked.

"Christmas is nothing but a scheme by stores to make suckers spend money. He'll be better off without a job!" Eddie said.

"But Principal Davis would kill us," Melody reminded him.

"I'm not afraid of him," Eddie said. "I'm not afraid of anyone."

5

A Jolly Disaster

By lunchtime, Eddie had already figured out a plan.

"I know how to get rid of Mr. Jolly," he announced at the lunch table.

"What are you going to do?" Howie asked.

"It's what WE'RE going to do," Eddie said. "I want you all to help me."

"I don't know," Howie said as he stuffed his mouth with a pickle. "Principal Davis caught us the last time I let you talk me into one of your dumb tricks."

"That was your own fault for putting the peanut butter jars in our trash can," Eddie said.

"I don't care," Howie said firmly. "I'm not helping this time."

"Me, neither," added Liza and Melody.

"Fine," Eddie snapped. "I don't need your help anyway. I'll do it myself."

When they were back in their classroom, Eddie raised his hand. "Mrs. Ewing, may I go to the bathroom?" he asked in a sickly sweet voice.

"I suppose," Mrs. Ewing said. "But hurry. We're getting ready to start the science lesson."

Eddie nodded seriously as he left the room.

Once he was in the hall Eddie acted fast. He dashed into the boys' bathroom and stuffed every roll of toilet paper under his shirt. "I look like a lumpy Santa," he laughed when he saw himself in the mirror.

Then he slipped back into the hall and started walking. I have to find the perfect place, he said to himself. Where they'd never suspect I'd been.

He peeked into the girls' bathroom but then shook his head. Too risky, he thought. A girl could walk in any minute.

He glanced at the clock hanging on the wall. It was halfway between lunch and the end of school. Every class in the building was busy trying to finish their day's work.

That's when it hit him. The perfect idea. He turned a corner and headed straight for the teachers' lounge.

Once inside he dumped his load of toilet paper and started to drape it over every piece of furniture. He stuffed wads inside the ditto machine and coffee maker. He even hung some from the lights by standing on a chair.

When he was finished, he looked at his work. "Perfect," he said. "This mess

ought to keep any janitor busy."

Before running back to his classroom, Eddie made a quick detour to the basement closet.

Mrs. Ewing was saying some stuff about solids and liquids when Eddie sailed into the room.

Eddie sat down and winked at Howie. "I turned the heat up, and that stupid janitor won't be turning it down anytime soon!" Eddie whispered.

"Why's that?" Howie whispered back.

"It'll take him three days just to clean up the mess I made in the teachers' room." Eddie couldn't help feeling proud of himself. And he was already feeling warmer.

"Eddie, did you want to say something to the class?" Mrs. Ewing interrupted.

"No, thanks," Eddie said loudly.

"Please pay attention to the lesson, then," Mrs. Ewing said as she began writing on the board.

"I've gotta see this," Howie whispered. Mrs. Ewing wasn't very happy when Howie asked to go to the bathroom, but she let him go anyway.

Howie was only gone a few minutes. He came back in the room shaking his head. "You liar," he whispered to Eddie. "There's no mess in the teachers' lounge. It's as clean as a whistle!"

"What?" Eddie tried to whisper. "I put toilet paper everywhere. There's no way Mr. Jolly could've cleaned it up that fast."

"There's nothing there now," Howie shrugged. "Nothing but Mr. Jolly."

"That can't be!" Eddie shivered. Was it his imagination, or was it already getting colder?

6

Checking It Twice

As soon as Mrs. Ewing dismissed them that afternoon, Eddie grabbed his friends in the hall.

"We've got to go to the teachers' lounge," Eddie said. "Something strange is happening."

"Oh, Eddie," Howie sighed. "Why don't you just admit you lied? You didn't do anything to the teachers' lounge."

"But I did," Eddie yelled. "And I'm going to find out who undid it!" Eddie turned and stomped toward the lounge.

Melody, Liza, and Howie looked at each other and then followed.

The lounge was full of teachers, drinking coffee as they tried to stay warm. But the four kids were able to peek inside long enough to see a sparkling clean room.

"Isn't that Mr. Jolly great?" they heard Mrs. Ewing say. "I just wish he wouldn't keep the building so cold."

"But this place has never been so clean," another teacher agreed. "I don't know how he does it!"

"It's almost like magic!" Mrs. Ewing said. "Speaking of magic, did you hear about the food drive? The box was over-

flowing with jars of peanut butter, and no one will admit to bringing them in!"

Eddie pulled away from the door. "Magic, my eyeball. That Mr. Jolly is nothing but a cold-blooded old geezer."

"Watch out," Melody warned Eddie. "He's standing right behind you."

Sure enough, Mr. Jolly had listened to every word they said. And he was writing in his little red notebook.

"Hello, boys and girls." Mr. Jolly smiled as he slipped his red notebook into a pocket. "I thought you kids would stay far away from the teachers' lounge!"

"Oh, we just had to show Eddie how clean it was," Liza blurted.

Eddie jabbed her in the ribs. "The lounge *is* awfully clean," Eddie muttered.

Mr. Jolly winked. "Let's keep it that way, too."

"It's not up to us to keep it clean," Eddie said.

Mr. Jolly rubbed his beard. "And it's not up to you to make the messes."

"Let's get out of here," Eddie said.

" 'Bye Mr. Jolly," Liza and Howie waved.

The four kids ran outside and met under the big oak tree.

"There's something weird about Mr. Jolly," Eddie announced.

"It is creepy the way he watches us," Melody agreed.

"And why is he always writing in that notebook?" Liza asked.

"It's like he's writing down everything we do," Howie added.

"Maybe he's a spy," Eddie teased.

Melody rolled her eyes. "Why would anyone want to spy on us?"

"He could be Santa Claus," Liza suggested quietly.

Eddie burst out laughing. "Liza, why don't you grow up?"

"Wait a minute," Howie interrupted. "Mr. Jolly does keep the building as cold as the North Pole."

"And what about the little man all dressed in green?" Melody added. "He could've been one of Santa's elves!"

"Didn't that little guy call him S.C.?" Liza asked. "That could be short for Santa Claus."

"You guys act like you're in kindergarten," Eddie sneered. "Santa Claus is kids' stuff!"

"Maybe you're right," Melody said. "After all, Santa Claus doesn't mop floors. And I've never seen Santa wearing shorts or green tennis shoes."

"How would you know?" Liza asked. "Maybe he's just pretending to be a janitor."

"Mr. Jolly is just an old man who's trying to turn us into Freeze Pops," Eddie said. "But I'm not going to let him!"

7

Let It Snow!

Eddie waited under the big oak tree the next morning. A few snowflakes whirled to the ground as Melody walked up. The grass was so cold it scrunched under her feet.

"I've got the perfect plan," Eddie said quickly.

"Plan for what?" Melody asked.

"A surefire plan to make Mr. Jolly Janitor forget all about turning down the heat," Eddie said firmly.

"He does keep the building awfully cold," Melody nodded.

"Then you'll help me?" Eddie asked.

"I don't know," Melody said. "What're you going to do?"

"Come on, I'll show you," Eddie said, and motioned for his friend to follow as he started walking toward the school.

"Why don't we wait for Liza and Howie?" Melody suggested.

"We have to act fast, before Mr. Jolly and everybody comes. Are you coming or not?"

Melody shivered. "I guess," she said reluctantly. She followed Eddie into the hallway and watched as he pulled five huge cans of whipped cream from his bookbag.

"What are you going to do with those?" Melody asked.

"Mr. Jolly likes it cold, right?" Eddie asked.

"Right," Melody agreed.

"We're going to give Mr. Jolly what he wants. We're going to make it snow in the halls!" Eddie grabbed a can in each hand and started squirting the walls.

"I don't think this is a good idea," Melody said as she watched.

"Don't be such a chicken," Eddie teased, "and start helping!"

"I'm no chicken," Melody snapped. She grabbed a can and wrote Mr. Jolly's name on the wall.

Eddie put one can down, squirted a mountain of whipped cream in his hand, and then slurped it up. "Hey! This makes a great breakfast."

Melody squirted a stream straight into her mouth. "Mmmmm, this is good," she said.

They took turns squirting heaps of snow-white whipped cream on the wall and then in their mouths. By the time they finished, the hall looked like it had been hit by a blizzard.

"This will keep Mr. Jolly so busy, he won't have time to think about the temperature," Eddie said.

"You're right," Melody agreed.

Eddie quickly threw all the empty cans into the second grade's trash can.

"Let's get out of here," Melody whispered. "I think I hear someone coming."

They both heard Mr. Jolly's keys jingling not too far away.

Eddie nodded. "Let's go turn up the heat. This mess is gonna keep Mr. Jolly busy all morning long."

Melody giggled. "I'm afraid he won't be so jolly when he sees this!"

Liza was just getting a drink from the water fountain when Melody and Eddie rushed to their classroom. Eddie went straight into the room, but Melody whispered to Liza about the whipped cream.

"I can't believe you'd do something so awful," Liza cried.

"It was only whipped cream," Melody said uneasily. "It's not like it was paint."

"Eddie is always doing something rotten," Liza said, wiping water off her mouth. "But I thought you were nice."

"I am nice," Melody snapped.

"I bet Mr. Jolly doesn't think so," Liza said.

"He doesn't know I did it," Melody said, slurping down a big gulp of water.

"What if he is Santa Claus?" Liza asked. "Santa Claus sees everything. Just like the song says, 'He sees you when you're sleeping, he knows — '"

"Mr. Jolly isn't Santa Claus," Melody insisted.

"Maybe not," Liza agreed. "But what if he is? Are you willing to take that chance?"

Melody shrugged her shoulders. "Oh, all right. I guess I could help clean up some of the mess."

"I'll help, too," Liza offered.

"You're really a good friend," Melody

said gratefully as they headed down the hallway.

Liza stopped in her tracks when she rounded the corner. "I thought this was where you put the whipped cream."

"It was," Melody said.

"There's nothing there now," Liza pointed.

Melody stared in disbelief. The wall was sparkling clean. Not one trace of whipped cream was anywhere to be seen.

"I don't get it," Melody said. "We used enough whipped cream to cover Wyoming. It would've taken Mr. Jolly all day to clean it up."

"Unless . . ." Liza said.

"Unless what?" Melody asked.

"Unless he really is Santa Claus," Liza whispered.

8

Magic?

"Eddie, I've got to tell you something," Melody whispered when she went into the room.

"Leave me alone," Eddie grumbled. "I don't feel very good."

"But I've got to tell you about Mr. Jolly," Melody insisted. "He's magic."

"What are you talking about?" Eddie said. His face looked greener than the

Christmas paper chains that decorated the room.

"Mr. Jolly cleaned up the whipped cream mess already," Melody whispered.

"Nobody could've cleaned it up that fast," Eddie muttered.

"Nobody but Santa," Melody whispered.

"Mr. Jolly may be fast, but he sure isn't Santa Claus. Even if there was a Santa Claus, he sure wouldn't be a big fat janitor." Eddie groaned and laid his head down.

"Maybe every year Santa Claus goes to a different school and gets to know the children there . . . ," Melody wondered out loud.

"Yeah," Eddie squeaked, "and maybe the Easter Bunny is the old lady that burns the hamburgers in the cafeteria."

"Eddie, I'm serious," Melody said.

"I'm serious, too," Eddie groaned. "I

ate too much whipped cream. I think I'm gonna be sick." Eddie ran up to the front of the room. Mrs. Ewing took one look at his face and sent him to the office.

"I'm sick," Eddie moaned when he got there.

"Too much whipped cream will make anyone sick," Mr. Jolly laughed from one side of the office. He was busy writing in his little red notebook.

"I haven't been eating any whipped cream," Eddie lied. "I think I may have the flu. I need to go home."

"I'll call your dad right away," the secretary told Eddie.

Eddie walked over to Mr. Jolly and tried to peek in his book. But Mr. Jolly snapped it shut and put it in his shorts pocket.

"What are you always writing about in that little red notebook?" Eddie asked.

"Oh, I like to notice things about people and write them down," Mr. Jolly said.

"In other words," Eddie said, "you're spying."

"I wouldn't exactly call it spying," Mr. Jolly said, smiling. "I just call it observing."

"Did you observe something about me?" Eddie asked.

"As a matter of fact, I did," Mr. Jolly said. "I noticed that you don't believe in Christmas or Santa Claus."

"Christmas is for little kids, and even if there was a Santa Claus, he couldn't bring me what I want for Christmas," Eddie said as he rubbed his aching stomach.

"And what is it you want — ?" Mr. Jolly started to ask. But before he finished, Eddie couldn't hold the whipped cream anymore. Out it came, along with most of Eddie's breakfast, all over Mr. Jolly's feet.

Mr. Jolly's big ring of keys jingled as

the secretary rushed Eddie to the bathroom.

In a few minutes, Eddie and the secretary came back into the office. Eddie looked like a sick walrus as he slumped into a chair.

The secretary didn't look too great, either. She glanced at Mr. Jolly's clean tennis shoes. "Didn't he . . . ?" She pointed. "Weren't those covered with . . . ?" The secretary shook her head. "Oh, never mind, I have to get in touch with Eddie's father."

"You can just forget about that," Eddie snapped. "He's not home and he won't be home until after Christmas."

"There has to be someone we can call," the secretary said.

"Maybe my grandmother will come get me," Eddie moaned. "If she isn't too busy."

Mr. Jolly sat down next to Eddie while

the secretary started dialing. "I'm sure your grandmother will come for you," Mr. Jolly said. "And when she does, you be sure to tell her you got sick on whipped cream."

"I told you I haven't eaten any whipped cream," Eddie insisted meekly.

Mr. Jolly chuckled as he stood up to leave. "I'm going to turn that heat down. And by the way, whipped cream doesn't look a thing like snow."

9

Ho! Ho! Ho!

"Don't you think it's weird?" Melody asked Eddie the next morning.

"What?" Eddie asked.

"That Mr. Jolly knew you wanted the whipped cream to look like snow?" Howie said.

"I'll tell you something else that's weird," Liza said. "The food drive box was filled with cans of whipped cream!"

They were all gathered around the water fountain the next morning. Eddie wasn't green anymore.

"I'm telling you," Liza insisted, "he's Santa Claus."

"She may be right," Melody agreed. "After all, have you ever heard of anybody named Jolly before?"

"And his initials are S.C.," Howie added.

Eddie kicked the wall. "S.C. probably just stands for sour cabbage," he grumbled. "I won't believe he's Santa Claus until I see him fly through the sky in his sleigh."

"Maybe we better be careful, just in case," Liza suggested.

"In case he really is Santa," Howie agreed.

"I do want lots of presents for Christmas," Melody added.

"You guys have slush for brains," Eddie interrupted. "I know Mr. Jolly isn't Santa Claus, and I'm going to prove it."

"How?" they all asked together.

"I'm going to follow him home after school," Eddie said.

"What will that prove?" Howie asked.

"When you see the dump Mr. Jolly lives in, it'll prove he's just an ordinary fat person. Anybody who's not a chicken will come with me!" Eddie dared.

That afternoon Eddie and Howie hid in the bathroom when the last bell rang.

"We've got to figure out a way to watch Mr. Jolly without him seeing us," Eddie said.

"That'll be impossible if he really is Santa Claus," Howie said.

Eddie rolled his eyes. "C'mon," he said, "let's wait in the oak tree until he leaves. Then we can follow him."

Howie grabbed Eddie's arm. "Don't we need to find Melody and Liza?"

"Naw," Eddie said, "they went home. I knew they'd be too chicken."

Howie and Eddie sneaked out of the building and into the freezing wind.

"Oh, it's colder than a penguin's nose out here," Eddie complained.

"We'll freeze if we stay here until Mr. Jolly gets finished. It'll take him a long time to clean the whole building," Howie whined.

"Do you want to find out the truth or not?" Eddie snapped.

"Not if it means turning into the Abominable Snowman," Howie said, shivering.

"Shut up and climb the tree," Eddie ordered.

The two boys sat on the icy branches and waited.

Howie's toes didn't have time to get cold. With a jingling of keys, Mr. Jolly came out of the building. He carried a big bag slung over his shoulders.

Howie elbowed Eddie in the ribs. "Look! He's carrying a bag of toys!"

Both boys watched as Mr. Jolly tossed the huge bag into the trash bin.

"No, frost face, it was only garbage," Eddie whispered.

Mr. Jolly took a deep breath and patted his bulging stomach. He lit his pipe and then jingled his keys again. As if by magic, a bright red sports car sped up.

The driver was so short he could barely see over the steering wheel. But the boys knew who it was as soon as they saw his green hat and pointy black beard. It was Eli.

Eli backed the shiny red car into the space in front of Mr. Jolly. That's when Howie noticed it. He jabbed Eddie and pointed. Even Eddie was speechless for once as he read the license plate. In green letters it said, "Ho! Ho! Ho!"

10

You Better Watch Out

"He really IS Santa Claus," Howie shrieked. Mr. Jolly and Eli turned to look at the oak tree.

"Shhh," Eddie hissed. "They'll hear you!" He reached across some branches to slap his hand over Howie's mouth. But Howie pulled back and Eddie ended up grabbing empty air.

"Ahhh!" Eddie screamed as he fell to the frozen ground.

Mr. Jolly and Eli came rushing over.

"Are you all right?" Mr. Jolly asked.

"I . . . I think so," Eddie stammered.

Eli helped Eddie to his feet. "There's another one up there, S.C.," he said as he pointed up to Howie.

Howie slithered down from the tree and

landed at Mr. Jolly's feet. "You are Santa Claus, aren't you?" Howie shouted.

Eli gasped, but Mr. Jolly just tugged at his beard. "Now, whatever gave you that idea?"

"I knew it!" Howie yelled. "See, Eddie, I told you so!"

Eddie stood up straight and stared hard at Mr. Jolly. "He never said he was. And even if he did, I wouldn't believe it!"

"What a rude little boy," Eli interrupted. "Really, S.C., I don't see why you put up with him."

Eddie turned to Eli. "I'd watch who you were calling *little*, mistletoe breath!"

Mr. Jolly put a hand on both of their shoulders. "Settle down, both of you."

Eli took a deep breath and let it out slowly. Howie could smell peppermint on his breath.

"I believe we should leave, S.C.," Eli

said quietly. "You've messed around with these kids long enough."

"You can't leave now, Santa!" Howie squeaked.

Mr. Jolly laughed, but not the way most grown-ups do. This laugh came from deep inside him. Then he puffed on his pipe, letting the smoke curl around his head. "Your friend doesn't seem to agree with you," he said as he nodded at Eddie.

"Eddie doesn't agree with anyone," Howie said. "But that doesn't mean anything!"

Eddie punched Howie on the arm. "I think you've got ice cubes for brains, and half of them are melted."

"See," Howie said. "He's just rotten."

Mr. Jolly shook his head. "Perhaps. Or perhaps he just needs Christmas spirit."

"Quit talking about me!" Eddie yelled. "You're nothing but a crazy fat man with a short friend. You're going to be sorry you ever saw Bailey Elementary School!" And then he stomped away.

11

Santa's Challenge

"Wait a minute," Howie yelled after Eddie. Howie had chased Eddie two blocks and was breathing hard when he finally caught up with him.

"What do you want?" Eddie screamed.

"Don't be mad at me," Howie squeaked. "I'm your friend."

"Some friend," Eddie grumbled. "Do you always go around telling people I'm rotten?"

"No," Howie said. "Please don't be mad, I've got to tell you something."

"What now?" Eddie asked.

"Santa, I mean Mr. Jolly, told me something." Howie's voice was almost in a whisper.

"What?" Eddie asked again.

Howie looked around to see if anyone

was listening. "He told me that we had our work cut out for us."

"What work?" Eddie asked impatiently.

"Making you believe in Christmas," Howie announced.

"I told you, Christmas is for little kids," Eddie snapped. "If my own father doesn't even care about Christmas, then why should I?"

"Because Christmas is a special time,"

Howie said softly. "Why, it's a time of believing in miracles. Isn't it a miracle that Santa Claus is at our school?"

"Miracles," Eddie sputtered. "I don't believe in miracles or Santa Claus. If Santa Claus can't make my father believe in Christmas, then there really isn't a Santa Claus and there sure aren't any miracles."

Howie shook his head sadly as Eddie stomped off. This time, Howie didn't follow him.

12

Santa's Miracle

"Brace yourself," Howie said as Eddie walked into the classroom the next morning. Mrs. Ewing was writing the assignments on the board.

Melody shook her head and whispered, "There's no telling what Eddie's going to do to poor Mr. Jolly today."

"You mean Santa Claus," Liza corrected.

"Eddie will blow his chances to ever celebrate Christmas if he does something terrible to Mr. Jolly, I mean Santa," Howie said.

They all got quiet as Eddie sat down. Eddie smiled but didn't say a word.

"Hi, Eddie," Howie said.

"Hi!" Eddie smiled back.

"Why are you so quiet this morning?" Melody asked.

"I can't tell you yet," Eddie said with a big smile on his face. "I have to see Mr. Jolly first."

Mrs. Ewing stopped writing on the board when she heard Eddie. "Children," she said, "I just found out that Mr. Jolly is gone. Principal Davis said Mr. Jolly called him late last night to tell him that he had to quit. It seems he found work up north."

"Oh, no!" Howie moaned. "Do we have to clean the building again?"

Mrs. Ewing smiled. "Luckily, Mr. Dobson has agreed to give us another try."

"Oh," Eddie said, "I wanted to tell Mr. Jolly something."

"What did you want to tell him?" Liza asked.

"I wanted to tell him thank you," Eddie said. "And I wanted to tell him I believe in miracles."

Mrs. Claus Doesn't Climb Telephone Poles

**Read more books
by Debbie Dadey
and Marcia Thornton Jones!**

Ghostville Elementary®

Mrs. Claus Doesn't Climb Telephone Poles

by Debbie Dadey
and
Marcia Thornton Jones

illustrated by John Steven Gurney

A
LITTLE APPLE
PAPERBACK

SCHOLASTIC INC.
New York   Toronto   London   Auckland   Sydney
Mexico City   New Delhi   Hong Kong   Buenos Aires

Contents

1. Blizzard of the Century   1

2. Liza's Wild Ride   7

3. Rotten Fruitcake   17

4. Abominable Snowman   27

5. Everywhere   34

6. The North Pole   41

7. The Abominable Snowman
   Strikes Again   46

8. Magic   55

9. Snowball Fight of the Century   63

10. Hot   68

11. Love Letter   73

12. A Package of Proof   78

Cool Holiday Puzzles and Activities   83

1

Blizzard of the Century

"Nothing is working," Eddie complained as he tossed his gloves on the snow-covered ground. "I couldn't call Howie last night and the Internet is down. What's going on?"

"It's all this snow," Liza told him. "The weatherman said it was the blizzard of the century. We haven't had this much snow in a hundred years."

Howie, Liza, Eddie, and Melody were gathered under the snow-laden branches of an old oak tree. "It's beautiful," Melody said, looking around at the huge piles of snow that covered everything — even their school.

"This blizzard is good for something," Eddie said with a grin. "School is closed until after Christmas."

1

Melody threw snow up in the air. The snow sprinkled back down onto her black braids. "We're free!" she cheered. "We can do anything we want!"

"At least until the streets are clear and they open school again," Liza reminded her friends.

"I want to work on my history report," Howie said. "I wonder when the Internet is going to be fixed."

"Forget history until after Christmas," Eddie said. "I want to use the Internet to be the first to squash the alien monster bugs in the Zirlot Space Invaders game."

"Maybe that lady is fixing it right now." Melody pointed to a short, stocky woman in red overalls working high up on a telephone pole. The woman waved to the kids. Liza, Melody, and Howie waved back. Eddie stuck out his tongue and crossed his eyes, but the lady was too far away to see him.

"Be nice," Liza warned. "That lady is working hard!"

"She doesn't look like any telephone repair person I've ever seen," Howie said. "She looks more like she should be baking cookies."

Melody crossed her arms over her chest. "What is that supposed to mean?" she snapped.

Howie shrugged. "Don't get mad at me," he said. "I know women can do anything. It's just that she looks more like my grandmother than a telephone repair person."

Liza giggled. "Grandmothers can climb telephone poles, too, you know."

"I don't care if she's Mother Goose," Eddie complained. "Let's stop talking about her and do something fun. I want to go over to Dedman Hill and go sledding!"

Liza gulped. Dedman Hill was the biggest, slipperiest sledding hill this side of the North Pole. "Why don't we just go home and drink hot chocolate?" Liza suggested. "Or we could make snow

4

angels." She flopped to the ground, then waved her arms and legs to make an angel.

"No way," Eddie said. "Let's meet at Dedman Hill in fifteen minutes." Eddie grabbed his gloves and followed Melody and Howie.

Liza lay on the ground and groaned. She really didn't want to sled on such a big hill. She started to get up but noticed that the woman on the telephone pole was talking into a receiver. Was it Liza's imagination or did the woman just say, "Ho, ho, ho"?

2

Liza's Wild Ride

"Holy Toledo!" Eddie yelled. "Look at that hill. It's awesome!"

Awesome was not the word that Liza would have chosen. Terrifying was more like it. "Do you think it's safe?" Liza whispered to Melody.

Melody nodded and looked up the huge snow-covered hill. Kids of every size and shape dotted the slope. Some were on sleds and some simply had trashcan lids or pieces of plastic. A few kids tried out snowboards.

"There's that lady again." Howie pointed at a shiny red truck pulling up beside a telephone pole. The woman's tool belt jangled as she hopped out of the driver's seat.

"Duck," Liza called. "She sees us looking at her."

Liza jumped behind a drift of snow, but her friends waved at the woman. "We don't have to hide," Eddie said. "We're not doing anything wrong."

Liza's face turned red. She stood up as the woman introduced herself. "Greetings," the woman said. She was dressed entirely in red. Even her boots, cap, and mittens were red. "My name is Joy. Those are some nice sleds you have. Of course, my favorite is the QT-10."

Melody's eyes lit up. "I saw that at the hardware store. It's the best!"

"It's also very expensive," Howie told her. "My mother said she'd buy a house in Tahiti before she'd buy a sled that cost that much."

Joy nodded. "It is expensive," she said. "I must admit that the L-B56 is pretty good, too, and it's a lot cheaper."

"How do you know so much about sleds?" Eddie asked.

8

The lady put her hand over her mouth. "Oops, I'd better get to work." She hustled away and climbed the telephone pole without saying another word.

"I wonder if she has the phone lines fixed yet," Howie said.

"We've wasted enough time blabbing," Eddie snapped. "I came to go sledding. Who's ready?"

Liza stared down at her boots. Eddie grabbed her arm and pulled. "Come on, Liza," Eddie said. "I'll race you."

Liza's face turned whiter than the snow. "I . . . I . . . I think I'll just watch for a while," she stammered.

Eddie took one look at Liza and started teasing her. "Liza's scared. Liza's a wimp."

"Cut it out," Melody told Eddie. "Liza doesn't have to go down the hill if she doesn't want to."

Eddie shrugged. "She'll miss out on all the fun if she doesn't."

Liza watched while Melody, Howie,

10

and Eddie pulled their sleds up the steep hill. They stood in line and waited for their turn. Then, one at a time, her friends zoomed down.

"Ya-hoo!" Howie screamed.

"Coooooool!" Melody yelled.

"Holy Toledo!" Eddie hollered.

Liza had to admit it did look fun — a lot more fun than standing at the bottom watching everyone else. She took a deep breath and trudged up the hill beside Melody.

"You don't have to do this," Melody told Liza.

"I want to," Liza said, even though her stomach was doing a dance.

"One, two, three, go!" Eddie shouted. Before Liza could change her mind, Eddie shoved her sled with a snow-crusted boot. Then he hopped on his sled and zoomed down alongside her. "I'm going to beat you!" Eddie screamed into the rushing wind.

Liza wasn't the least bit interested in

winning a downhill race against Eddie. She was too worried about surviving the trip. Liza closed her eyes as she whisked down the hill. "Helpppppppp!" she screamed.

Liza opened her eyes in time to see Eddie slip behind her. Everything was a blur as she whipped along. Finally, she reached the bottom of the hill and coasted to a stop.

Liza stood up with trembling knees and looked around for her friends. Eddie had stopped halfway up the hill and lots of other kids were close to him. She was the only one to make it all the way to the bottom.

At the top of the hill, Melody put her hands around her mouth and yelled, "Way to go, Liza! You won! You won!"

Eddie wasn't cheering. He stood up and kicked his sled. He didn't even look at Liza, but pushed his way back up the hill and to the front of the line.

"Hey," Melody told Eddie. "Just because

Liza went farther than you, doesn't mean you have to get mad."

"I'm not mad," Eddie snapped. "And I don't have to listen to you — or to anyone else. I can do whatever I want."

Liza climbed to the top of the slope and noticed that Joy was now on the telephone pole just behind a nearby spruce tree. Liza could hear Joy's tools jangling, but that wasn't all she heard. Liza was sure she heard Joy say "ho, ho, ho" into a phone line.

Liza pulled Melody away from the line of kids. Howie and Eddie came over to see what was going on. "I just heard Joy say 'ho, ho, ho,'" Liza told them. "She said it before, too."

Eddie rolled his eyes. "Big deal. Anyone can say 'ho, ho, ho.' See? Ho, ho, ho, ho," he said, just to prove his point.

Liza ignored Eddie. "Isn't it strange how the telephone lady just appeared after the big blizzard?" she said. "It's almost like she *blew* into town."

Melody patted Liza's shoulder. "I think we need to get you out of the cold. You're starting to sound a little flaky."

"How about we *blow* into Burger Doodle for some hot chocolate?" Howie suggested. "My hands are freezing."

Eddie nodded. "Let's sled down one more time first."

"Not me," Liza said. "One wild ride a day is enough. I'm walking down."

"What?" Eddie snapped. "You have to race me again."

"Not today," Liza said.

Eddie didn't want to give up. "Then when?" he asked.

Liza rubbed her hands together to keep them warm. "Next Saturday."

"That's Christmas Eve," Eddie complained. "It's too far away!"

Liza didn't answer Eddie. She started walking down the hill. Secretly she hoped all the snow would melt before next Saturday. It had been exciting to sled down Dedman Hill once, but she

15

wasn't sure she ever wanted to try it again.

"Wait a minute!" Eddie yelled. He ran to catch up with Liza and tripped in the thick snow. Instead of sledding down the hill, Eddie slid down on the seat of his pants. "Ahhhhh!" he screamed.

Melody giggled. "Now, *that's* one wild ride."

3

Rotten Fruitcake

As soon as Eddie slid to a stop he was off and running. "Last one to Burger Doodle is a rotten fruitcake!" he screamed over his shoulder.

"Too late!" Melody yelled, taking off after him. "You're already the most rotten fruitcake of all!"

Melody was almost even with Eddie when he cut in front of her, forcing her to stumble into a pile of snow. "No fair!" Melody hollered as Eddie zipped around a corner toward Burger Doodle.

"All's fair in racing and war!" Eddie called back.

Melody stomped in a slush puddle. "That Eddie can be a real pain in the neck," she said when Howie and Liza

finally caught up to her. "He wouldn't even wait for his friends!"

"You didn't wait for us, either," Howie pointed out.

Melody didn't answer. She couldn't. Eddie popped around the corner and lobbed a snowball at her. It slammed right into Melody's knees. Snow dribbled down inside her boot.

"I'll get you for that!" Melody shouted. Off she ran, chasing Eddie right to the door of Burger Doodle Restaurant. Bells over the door jangled as Melody, Liza, and Howie followed Eddie inside.

"Beat you!" Eddie said with a grin as he rushed to be first in line.

"You cheated," Melody told him. "It doesn't count."

Eddie didn't pay any attention to Melody. As soon as he got his hot chocolate and a giant chocolate chip cookie, Eddie hurried across the restaurant so he could be the first to slide into a booth. When his friends were seated, he stuffed the entire cookie in his mouth. "I beat everyone," he said, only he was hard to understand because his mouth was full of cookie crumbs.

Liza rolled her eyes. Howie ignored him. Melody pointed her finger at Eddie's nose. "You are being very rude," she told him.

Liza nodded. "Everything doesn't have to be a race, you know."

"You're just saying that because you're a slowpoke," Eddie told Liza. "And I plan to prove it next Saturday when we race down Dedman Hill. Too bad I don't have a QT-10 or an L-B56."

"Those new sleds could be dangerous," Liza said after taking a sip of hot chocolate. "I think racing down Dedman Hill is dangerous."

"Liza's right," Howie said. "Maybe racing isn't such a good idea."

Melody glared at Eddie. "If Liza doesn't want to race, she doesn't have to."

Eddie wadded up a napkin and threw it at Melody. "Quit being such a goody-goody," he said. The napkin missed Melody, sailing over her head and right into the path of a short man dressed entirely in green.

"Pardon me," the man said. He quickly bent down, picked up the napkin, and handed it back to Eddie.

"You almost beaned a perfect stranger," Melody snapped at Eddie when the man walked away. "You're getting on everyone's nerves."

"He's not a stranger," Liza said softly. "I know him from somewhere. I just can't remember where."

Melody and Eddie were too busy bickering to hear her. Liza leaned around the corner of the booth and watched the short man as he made his way around tables and chairs to the back of the dining room. Liza gasped when she saw where he was heading.

"What's wrong?" Howie asked.

"That man," she said. "He's here to talk to Joy."

There, in the back booth, sat the woman who had been working on the telephone lines. She slowly stirred a cup of hot cider with a candy cane.

"So?" Eddie asked. "Who cares?" He took a sip of hot chocolate and ended up with a big brown mustache.

"Shh," Liza said. "I wonder what they're talking about."

"Only one way to find out," Eddie said. He slid down in his seat and crawled out from under the table. "Follow me," he whispered.

"Eddie," Melody warned, "it's not nice to spy on people."

Eddie didn't hear her. He was already halfway across the dining room. "We better go with him to make sure he doesn't cause any trouble," Liza said. She slid out of the booth. Howie looked at Melody and shrugged before following his two friends. Melody sighed. Sitting all alone in the booth didn't sound like much fun at all. She followed her friends.

Eddie had plopped down in the booth right behind Joy and the little man dressed in green. Liza, Howie, and Melody quietly sat down next to Eddie.

"Ho, ho, ho," Joy said to the little man. Only Joy didn't sound happy at all.

"Everyone at the shop is worried," the man said. "Will you tell me what happened?"

Joy took a deep breath. "I'm going to level with you. S.C. made me mad. He doesn't even remember to say good morning half the time. He's always busy, busy, busy. Sure, he's a jolly old soul, but sometimes I wish he would stop all that belly laughing and notice the work I've been doing. After all, if it wasn't for me, he wouldn't have his lists organized on the computer. And who keeps the workers'

schedule straight? Me, that's who. But, do I get any credit? No! Not even a thank-you. Nobody appreciates a single thing I do. Especially S.C.!"

"Haven't we seen that man somewhere before?" Liza whispered to her friends.

Howie quickly peeked over the top of the booth. "He does look familiar," he agreed.

"I need time away," Joy was saying. "Besides, S.C. is so busy he'll never miss me."

"That's not true," the man in green said. "He misses you. Everyone does. Production is down and no one feels like working. We won't meet our deadline without you. You must fly home before it's too late!"

Joy pulled a big red hanky from the pocket of her overalls and blotted her eyes. "If S.C. really misses me, then he'll come get me himself, Eli," she said.

Just then, Liza let out a scream that brought the entire restaurant to a complete standstill.

4

Abominable Snowman

All eyes turned to the booth where the four kids sat. The other customers looked at the kids for a full thirteen seconds. Then they turned back to their food.

"Whew," Howie said. "That was a close call."

"Let me tell you something about the spying business," Eddie said under his breath. "It's a good idea not to scream or yell or do dances on tables. That tends to blow your cover."

Liza leaned toward the center of the table and waited for her friends to huddle close. "Didn't you hear what Joy called that man in green?" Liza whispered. "Eli!"

"So?" Melody and Howie asked at the same time.

Liza's eyes were wide as she helped them remember. "Eli was the same man we saw talking to that janitor we had for a while. Remember? The janitor who turned out to be Santa Claus."

"We never proved that janitor was really Santa," Howie pointed out.

"Howie is right," Melody said. "He was probably just a fat man who was good with a mop."

"He was Santa Claus," Liza said. "I'm sure of it. And Eli is Santa's helper. That means Joy must be from the North Pole, too!"

Eddie looked at Liza, crossed his eyes, and put two straws in his mouth for fangs. "Yes, and I'm the Abominable Snowman," he said with a goofy grin.

"You're half right." Melody giggled. "You're definitely abominable!"

Liza was ready to argue, but a long shadow suddenly blocked the sun shining through the restaurant's windows. Liza shivered and looked right up into

Joy's blue eyes. The kids had been so busy talking they hadn't noticed that Eli had left the restaurant.

"Well, I see you four have come in off the slopes," Joy said. "How about a candy cane?"

"All right," Eddie cheered, reaching for the candy.

"Thank you, but we aren't allowed to take candy from strangers," Liza said politely, pulling Eddie's hand away.

Joy put her hands to her rosy cheeks. "Oh, you are so right! Up north, everyone knows me."

"We saw you working on the telephone poles," Howie said. "Do you like it?"

Eddie stood up on his seat so he towered over his friends. "Climbing poles would be fun. Have you ever tried tying a rope to the top for a giant swing?"

Joy giggled and her blue eyes sparkled. "Oh, my. That wouldn't be a smart thing to do, now would it?"

Eddie opened his mouth to answer but

snapped it shut. Joy had tricked him into being speechless.

"Climbing poles is fun, but it's also hard work," Joy said, not seeming to notice Eddie's silence. "I'm pretty good at it, if I do say so myself. I've been making and fixing things for as long as I can remember."

"I wish I could fix things," Eddie blurted. "Then maybe I could fix my favorite toy."

Joy clapped her hands. "I do enjoy toys, even though I haven't been a child for centuries. What is your favorite toy?"

Eddie puffed out his chest. "It's a giant Bug Squasher action figure from the Planet Zirlot. It has twelve legs and laser beams for eyes. I broke it by accident last week."

"I know all about Bug Squashers from Zirlot," Joy said. "I especially like the way their heads twirl in circles. If you like those, then I bet you'd really enjoy the hottest new action figure — the new, improved, super-duper Bug Squasher Z-Model."

Eddie jumped out of his seat. "Of course I would. I really want one. Every kid wants one. I bet I get a Z-Model for Christmas."

Joy's eyes sparkled. "That all depends, now doesn't it?" she said softly.

"Joy is right. You better not get your hopes up," Melody said, patting Eddie on the arm. "They've been sold out for weeks."

"The only person who could get a Z-Model this close to Christmas is Santa Claus himself," Howie added.

Liza nodded. "Of course Santa could get one. Santa can do anything, can't he?"

Joy cleared her throat and her eyes lost their sparkle. She looked at the four friends sitting in the booth. Then, without another word, Joy turned and ran out of Burger Doodle. The bells over the door jingled long after she was gone.

5

Everywhere

"No," the clerk told Eddie. "We sold out of that toy at least two months ago."

"Rats," Eddie said. "I've been to every place in town and it's the same story."

The kids were in the toy department of Dover's Department Store. It was the day after they had been sledding. Snow still coated the streets and sidewalks. "I told you they were sold out," Melody said to Eddie. Howie ignored all his friends. He was busy looking at a microscope. Howie wanted to be a doctor someday and was always interested in anything having to do with medicine or science.

The clerk shrugged his shoulders and walked away. "Maybe you could try asking Santa."

"Or Mrs. Claus," Melody said with a giggle.

"Look," Liza said, interrupting her friends. The kids turned around to see Joy talking with another salesclerk.

"Now, personally," Joy was saying, "I wouldn't recommend the Suzy Kellogg Egg Fryer for anyone under five, but the Mickey Flip-Flop Fryer is safe for any age."

The clerk nodded and asked, "What do you think about the Deluxe Doggy Doo-Doo Maker?"

Joy giggled. "That's the silliest toy I've ever seen. I hope parents aren't crazy enough to buy it for their little darlings."

The clerk laughed while Joy threw her head back and belted out a loud, "Ho, ho, ho."

Later that week, the kids were at the Bonsai Bakery. Melody had to pick up a cake because her aunt was coming for Christmas Eve dinner. Nobody was be-

hind the counter, so Eddie rang the bell for service. *Ring. Ring. Ring.* "Come on," Eddie snapped. "We don't have all day."

"Eddie," Liza told him. "You should have more patience."

"Patience, smatience," Eddie said. "I have things to do."

Howie nodded. "Yeah, like our history report."

Eddie rolled his eyes. History and bakeries were definitely not what he had in mind, but he couldn't help drooling as he stared at the sugar cookies and butterscotch drops behind the counter.

"There's the problem," Melody said. Through the doorway, the kids saw Joy chatting with the owner.

"That lady is everywhere," Eddie snapped. "Why doesn't she climb back up a telephone pole and stay there?"

"Shh," Liza said. "Let's listen."

"Yes," Joy was saying. "Five cups of sugar and not one bit more. Those cookies will be perfect."

That wasn't the last time the kids saw Joy that week. When the kids were at the mall with Eddie's grandmother, they saw Joy in Fred Barbo's Sportarama. "That lady is starting to give me the creeps," Melody said.

"She's everywhere," Howie agreed.

"What's she up to now?" Liza asked.

"Come on," Eddie said. "Let's find out."

The kids sneaked up behind a big canoe to listen. "This is a good coat," Joy told a customer.

"Do you work here?" the man asked.

"Oh, heavens no," Joy said. "But where I come from it's very cold. I know a good coat when I see one. I've made plenty in my day."

The customer nodded and walked away with the coat. Liza stood up and waved to Joy. "Greetings," Joy said, holding up a scarf. "What a pleasure to see you."

"Are you shopping for your husband?"

Liza asked. Howie, Melody, and Eddie stood up beside the canoe.

"I do have half a mind to get a scarf for my husband. He's always so busy getting presents for everyone else, going over his lists, and checking them twice. A scarf would be the perfect thing for him. I can never get him to wear one and his nose stays as red as a cherry gumdrop," Joy said.

"You must really care about your husband to worry about his nose," Howie said.

"Of course I care about him," Joy said. "But do you think he'd give one thought about my nose? Of course not. He's too busy for that." Joy folded the scarf and plopped it back on the shelf. "Excuse me, children. I want to talk to this clerk about those new sleds."

Liza stared at Joy as she walked away. Something about what Joy said bothered Liza. She just couldn't figure out what it was.

6

The North Pole

"You have to come with me," Liza told her friends on the morning of Christmas Eve. They were standing under the oak tree, trying to warm their hands. The wind whistled through the tree branches and little snowflakes danced in the air.

"No way," Eddie snapped. "You promised me we'd have a sled race today and you're not going to get out of it."

Liza gulped. She didn't really want to race down that huge hill again, and right now she had more important things on her mind. She'd been thinking about Joy all week. "I'll go sledding right after we do this one thing," she told her friends. "I promise."

"Oh, let's just go with her," Melody said. "She won't stop asking until we do."

Howie shrugged. "I'll go."

Earlier, on her way to the oak tree, Liza had seen Joy up a telephone pole at the corner of Main and Forest Lane. The kids got to the corner just in time to see Joy walking away. "Come on," Liza whispered. "We don't want to lose her."

Eddie grumbled. "I can't believe I'm chasing a grandma down the street when I could be sledding."

"Eddie," Liza said softly. "This is important." The kids followed Joy down Main Street and past Howie's house. Joy turned off Main Street onto a little gravel road. The street sign said SNOWFLAKE LANE.

"I've never been this way before," Howie said. "I wonder what's down here." Howie didn't have to wonder for long. The kids passed a grove of towering pine trees and came into a clearing just in time to see Joy enter a small cottage.

"Oh, it's adorable," Melody said.

"It looks like the house from *Hansel and Gretel,*" Liza admitted.

Eddie rubbed his stomach and mumbled, "I wonder if I can eat it."

"Only if you want to get electrocuted," Howie pointed out. "Look at all those lights."

Twinkling Christmas lights outlined the roof, the door, and every window. All around the house, spruce trees and bushes glittered with lights and ornaments. Bright red-and-white candy canes lined the brick sidewalk. A giant snowman smiled down at the kids from the roof.

Eddie laughed out loud. "This house looks like something from the North Pole. I wish my dad didn't travel so much. Then he'd have time to put up lights like this."

Liza stared at Eddie. "What did you say?" she asked.

"I said, I wish my dad would put up Christmas lights," Eddie said.

Liza shook her head. "No, what else did you say?"

Eddie was tired of looking at lights. "Stop wasting time," he said. "You promised you'd sled today. So let's get going." Eddie jogged away without waiting for an answer.

Liza took one more look at the little cottage on Snowflake Lane. There was something very mysterious about it. She just wished she could figure out what it was. Unfortunately, she didn't have time to think. Right now, she had to risk her life on Dedman Hill.

7

The Abominable Snowman Strikes Again

As usual, Eddie beat his friends to Dedman Hill. He leaned his sled against a tree at the base of the hill and hoisted himself up to a low branch. Eddie had a perfect view of all the action.

Eddie wasn't the only one with a good view. Joy was high up a nearby telephone pole. Her tool belt jangled as she perched near the top and worked on the lines.

Several kids were slowly climbing the steep slope. A small boy at the top peered over the edge of the hill, then took a step back in fear. Eddie would never be afraid to zip down the slope. He couldn't wait to show every kid in Bailey City how fast he could go. Especially Liza.

As soon as Howie, Liza, and Melody were under Eddie's tree, he roared, "The Abominable Snowman strikes again!" Then Eddie shook the tree limb. An avalanche of snow fell right on his friends' heads.

"Eddie, you are worse than the Abominable Snowman," Melody said, shaking snow from her braids.

Liza giggled and wiped snow from Howie's back. "I bet the Abominable Snowman would run from Eddie."

"He couldn't outrun me and my super-slide sled," Eddie bragged. "It can go faster than a snow monster and anyone else on this hill. I bet I can ride faster than Santa's sleigh!"

Melody rolled her eyes. "Bragging doesn't make it true," she told Eddie. "It only means you're the biggest pest on this hill."

Eddie jumped down and faced Melody, nose to nose. "You don't think I'm the fastest one here?"

Melody took one step back. "I know you're not the fastest because Liza beat you last week," she told Eddie. "You might as well face it. Liza is faster than you."

Eddie's face turned red, and it wasn't just from the cold wind. "I wasn't trying to win that day!" Eddie said before stomping up the hill.

"Eddie needs to learn that winning isn't everything," Melody said. "And I'm just the one to teach him. Let's go!"

The three friends followed Eddie. Their boots sunk deep in the snow and their breath made tiny white clouds. As soon as they reached the top, Eddie shoved aside two kids to get to the front of the line.

"Wait your turn," Melody said.

"I don't have time to wait," Eddie snapped. "This hill has my name on it."

"That's it!" Melody snapped. "I've had enough of your abominable behavior." Melody was so mad, she stomped away.

Eddie didn't care. He was determined

to prove that he had the fastest sled on the hill. He dropped his sled at the top of the hill. Then he stood on top of it.

"Eddie!" Liza yelped. "Get down before you hurt yourself!"

Eddie grinned and held his hands high over his head. "I am the future gold-medal winner of the Dedman Hill Olympics!" he hollered.

Unfortunately, the sled started moving through the snow while he was in the middle of his victory cheer.

"Watch out!" Howie warned.

Too late. The sled slipped out from under Eddie. He fell into a deep pile of snow. His sled zoomed down the hill without him. "NOOOOOOOOOO!" Eddie screamed as his sled headed straight for the tree at the bottom of the hill. It smacked into the tree and broke into three pieces.

"My sled! My sled!" Eddie cried out. "No fair!"

Melody shook her hand in Eddie's

direction. "You're lucky you didn't crack your head," she told him.

Howie helped Eddie out of the snow-drift. He was covered in snow from the top of his curly red hair to the bottom of his black boots.

"Now you really do look like the Abominable Snowman," Liza said with a giggle.

"It's not funny," Eddie said. "My sled's broken into smithereens. This is the worst Christmas Eve ever!"

Eddie sat on the ground and slid all the way down the hill on the seat of his pants. Howie and Melody zipped by him on their sleds. Liza peered down the hill after her friends. Down, down, down they went. The longer they slid, the more her stomach tumbled. She decided to walk down the hill instead of sliding.

Just as Liza reached the bottom, Joy shimmied down a nearby telephone pole to join the kids. They were trying to put Eddie's sled back together again.

"Looks like you had an accident," Joy said to Eddie.

"It wasn't my fault," Eddie told her, holding up a piece of his sled. "It just took off on its own. Now my sled is ruined."

Joy kneeled down to examine the damage. "Well, now," she said. "I wouldn't say it's ruined. It just needs a few screws tightened." Joy whipped a screwdriver from her belt and bent over the sled. She worked so fast, Liza had a hard time following Joy's hands. "There you go," Joy said suddenly. "All fixed."

"Wow!" Eddie said with a low whistle. "I was sure this sled was toast, but you made it look good as new!"

"My husband and I can fix just about anything," Joy said. "We've had lots of practice."

"What kind of job does your husband have?" Melody asked.

Joy laughed from deep in her belly. "You might say he's into toys," she said.

Then her smile faded. "They're his whole life. Even more important than me."

"How can I ever thank you?" Eddie asked as he ran his hands over his sled. For some reason, it looked shinier than before. "I'll do anything!"

"I hope you mean that," Joy said. "Because I know just the thing."

8

Magic

Joy smiled and patted Eddie on the head. "This is what you must do for me. From now on, I want you to be more careful. Just think how your family would feel if you got hurt."

Eddie thought for a moment. Then he nodded. "My grandmother would be upset if something happened to me. Who would she bake cookies for? Who would she buy toys for? Who would she read to at night?"

Melody sighed. "I would miss my mom and dad if I had to be away from them for a while. They would miss me, too."

"My family plays board games and cards every Friday night," Liza said. "I would miss that."

Howie nodded. "I would miss the way

my dad can turn doing the dishes into a science experiment."

Joy put her hand over her heart. Tears puddled in her blue eyes. "I must admit, all this talk of family makes me miss my husband."

"Where is your husband?" Howie asked.

"He's up north," she told him. "And all this beautiful snow reminds me of our little cottage nestled amidst the snowdrifts and glaciers."

The more Joy talked, the quieter Liza became. Not Eddie. He grew more restless. He stomped his foot, splattering them all with snow.

"All this snow reminds me of the race that's waiting for me at the top," Eddie interrupted. Then he looked right at Liza. "It's now or never," he said. "Get your sled, Liza. We have a date with Dedman Hill!"

Liza's mouth was suddenly dry. She tried to swallow. Her knees started shaking and she sat down hard in the snow.

"Are you too chicken?" Eddie asked.

"Leave her alone," Melody warned. "She doesn't have to sled down Dedman Hill if she doesn't want to."

Joy looked up at the top of the hill. Then she looked down at Liza. "I used to be quite a sledder back in my day," Joy said. "I have a great idea. How about if you and I go down together?"

"That might make it easier," Liza admitted. "Would you mind?"

"Mind? Of course not. I think it sounds absolutely marvelous."

Marvelous was putting it mildly. At the top of the hill, Joy hopped on the sled behind Liza and pushed off. Liza's sled quickly became a blur. They went so fast it looked like the sled's runners flew over the top of the snow. Liza didn't feel the least bit scared with Joy behind her.

Eddie stomped his feet and huffed into the cold air. "No fair. I want to go that fast."

Eddie didn't need to be mad. As soon

as Joy climbed to the top of the hill, she hopped on Eddie's sled. Together, Joy and Eddie flew down the steep slope. In fact, Joy rode with everyone.

"Wow," Melody said. "Every sled Joy rides seems to soar over the snow."

Howie's ears were tipped in red from the cold. He pulled his hat down over them. "It's almost like winter magic," he said.

Liza's eyes widened and her face turned as white as the snow on her mittens. "What did you say?" Liza asked.

"It just seems odd that the sleds go so fast when she's on them," Howie explained.

"Exactly," Liza said. She grabbed Howie's and Melody's coat sleeves and pulled them away from the rest of the kids on the hill. Eddie noticed his friends whispering. He hated the idea of losing his place in line, but he hated being left out of a secret even more. He scuffed through the snow to see what they were talking about.

"There's something very unusual about Joy," Liza was saying.

Eddie nodded. "She's fun," he said. "She hasn't forgotten how to play."

"That's because," Liza said slowly, "Joy has had lots of practice."

Melody pulled Liza's hat down over her ears. "Have your brains frozen?" she asked. "You're not making any sense."

Liza pushed Melody's hand away from her hat. "I'm making perfect sense. Joy has had lots of practice playing because she is the one and only Mrs. Santa Claus!"

Melody giggled. Howie smiled. Eddie plopped down in the snow and laughed out loud. "I'm pretty sure Santa's wife has better things to do than fix telephone wires," Eddie said.

"Eddie's right," Howie said. "The North Pole is far away. Why would Mrs. Claus want to vacation in Bailey City?"

"After all," Melody added, "I'm pretty

sure Mrs. Claus doesn't climb telephone poles."

"You have to believe me," Liza said. "I have it all figured out. Santa and Joy had a misunderstanding. It's up to us to get them back together. If we don't, something terrible might happen!"

9

Snowball Fight
of the Century

"Who cares?" Eddie told Liza.

Howie rubbed his gloves together to stay warm and nodded. "Eddie has a point. Even if Joy is the one and only Mrs. Claus, what difference would it make to us?"

Liza stomped her foot and looked at Eddie. "What if Joy tells Santa's elves everything that happens in Bailey City, including who's naughty or nice?"

"I'm not worried," Eddie said. "I'm not naughty."

Howie laughed and Liza shook her head. "You *should* be worried," Liza told Eddie.

"You're not exactly nice all the time," Melody pointed out.

"Eddie knows how to be good," Howie said in defense of his friend.

Liza nodded. "Good at trouble," she added.

"No," Eddie argued. "This city would be boring without me because I'm good at stirring up excitement. And that's exactly what I plan to do right now." Eddie scooped up a big snowball and tossed it at Liza. Soon he was throwing snowballs at everyone on the hill.

"Eddie, will you please listen to me?" Liza yelled as she ducked a snowball.

"I'm tired of listening," Eddie said. "We're kids. We're supposed to have fun!"

A girl named Becky tossed a big snowball at Eddie and hit him right on the mouth. Eddie spit out snow and shouted, "Look out! It's the snowball fight of the century!" He tossed snowballs like a catapult. Kids dived onto the snow-covered ground to avoid getting hit.

"Eddie, quit acting so crazy," Melody yelled, but Eddie didn't listen. When a

kid named Huey wasn't looking, Eddie put ice down Huey's shirt.

Melody tried to grab Eddie's coat to stop him, but he put snow in a kindergartner's mitten anyway. "Now that was downright mean," Melody snapped.

"I'm just having fun," Eddie said. "You need to stop being so grouchy."

"And you need to be nicer," Melody said as she ducked a snowball. Eddie didn't quit throwing snowballs, so Melody gave up trying to stop him. In fact, Melody threw a few snowballs of her own. Kids all over the top of Dedman Hill joined in the snowball fight.

Eddie was having a great time. What he didn't know was that Joy was watching. Liza knew. She had ducked behind a snow-laden spruce tree to avoid one of Eddie's snowballs. That's when Liza noticed Joy watching every snowball Eddie lobbed into the air. Joy shook her head each time Eddie did something not so nice.

"I have to tell Eli about this," Liza overheard Joy mutter out loud. With a jingle of her tool belt, she shimmied up a nearby telephone pole, whipped out her headset, and tapped into the telephone line.

"Ho, ho, ho," Joy said loud enough for Liza to hear. "Eli, there's something you should know before you leave tonight. Something important!"

10

Hot

After all that snowball throwing, Eddie needed a rest. "Let's head to Burger Doodle!" he shouted.

A huge group of kids followed Eddie down Forest Lane. They threw a few snowballs along the way but calmed down as they went inside Burger Doodle. "I want hot chocolate," Eddie told Skip, the counter worker.

"I'd like a Doodlegum Shake, please," Liza said. Melody and Howie got shakes, too. After the friends had their drinks, they headed to a booth against the back wall. Liza told her friends what she had overheard.

"Big deal," Eddie said. "It's not against the law to make a phone call, even if it is from the top of a pole."

Eddie took a big gulp of his hot chocolate and immediately spit it out all over the table. "Eddie," Melody shrieked. "That's disgusting." Howie grabbed some napkins and wiped up the table.

Eddie stuck out his tongue and fanned it. "Hot!" he whined. "My tongue is on fire!"

Liza giggled and gave Eddie a sip of her cold shake. "That's why it's called HOT chocolate," she said.

When Eddie had finally calmed down, Liza got serious. "We have to help Santa and Joy make up," she said. "If we don't, Santa might be too sad to deliver presents. There won't be a single toy under our trees tomorrow."

Howie shrugged. "I'm not sure Joy is Mrs. Claus, but even if she isn't, it would be nice to help her make up with her husband."

"It would be romantic," Melody agreed.

"Sounds disgusting to me," Eddie said, before carefully sipping his hot choco late. "Besides, do I look like Cupid to you?"

Liza looked at Eddie. He had a chocolate mustache, and chocolate was splattered all over his blue coat. His red baseball cap had snow on the bill and freckles dotted his cheeks. He definitely did *not* look like Cupid.

"Besides," Eddie continued. "Joy is fun and knows how to fix practically everything. She knows all about the hottest toys."

"That's because she gets the inside scoop from Santa," Melody interrupted.

Eddie ignored Melody. "If we help her get back with her husband," Eddie continued, "then she would leave Bailey City. I want her to stay here."

Liza pointed her finger at Eddie. "You can't be selfish about this. Joy deserves to be happy."

"Shh," Melody said. "I think Joy is right behind us."

The kids grew very quiet, except for

Eddie, who slurped the last of his hot chocolate. From the booth behind them, the kids heard Joy talking to Eli. "S.C. is upset," Eli told Joy. "Nothing has gone right since you left. The workers aren't organized. The lists are mixed up. There isn't a single butterscotch drop to be found. There's no way we can meet our midnight deadline at this rate. You have to come home before it's too late!"

"Did you hear that?" Liza whispered. "Christmas will be ruined and it will be Eddie's fault."

"My fault?" Eddie snapped. "What did I do?"

"You have to choose. Either be selfish or help us save Christmas for everyone," Liza said. "What will you do?"

11

Love Letter

"I'll help," Melody and Howie said at once. Then all three kids looked at Eddie.

"Okay," Eddie muttered and crushed his hot chocolate cup into a ball. "I'll help."

Liza smiled and leaned close to whisper. "This is what I have in mind. Melody, you're in charge of flowers. Howie, you need to send Joy candy. I'll make a big heart. Eddie, you can write Joy a love letter."

"What?" Eddie shouted. "There's no way I'm going write a 1...1...*l-o-v-e* letter!" Eddie spelled the word so he wouldn't have to say it. He stood up and started to walk way.

Liza looked ready to cry. "You just don't want to help us."

"Eddie never wants to help," Melody said. "He only cares about himself."

"This isn't about friendship. It's about insanity!" Eddie snapped, but he grew quiet when Joy put her hand on his shoulder.

"Is everything all right?" Joy asked.

"Eddie was just talking about a writing a love letter," Melody said with a grin.

A smile formed on Joy's face. "Aren't you kids a little young to be in love?" she asked.

Eddie's face got red all the way to the tips of his ears. He threw his baseball cap on the floor. "I am not in LOVE!" Eddie shouted. Everyone in the restaurant stopped sipping. They quit munching. They stopped talking. They all looked at Eddie. One kid named Ben laughed and started singing, "Eddie's in love! Eddie's in love!"

"Hush," Joy told him. Surprisingly, Ben sat down and got quiet. The rest of the kids went back to talking to their friends.

"Now look what you've done," Eddie fussed at Liza. "Ben will probably tease me for the rest of my life!"

Melody jumped up, put her hands on her hips, and stuck out her jaw. "It's not our fault," she told Eddie. "You're the one who has been acting mean, mean, mean!"

"You're not my friend anymore," Eddie told Melody. "None of you are!"

Liza hopped in front of Eddie before he could leave. "Don't go away mad, Eddie," she said. "We can talk this out. Friendship is too important to waste on a misunderstanding."

Joy nodded her head. "After all," she said, "everyone has arguments, but true friends have to make up and find a way to get along. Friendship isn't always easy, but it's definitely worth saving."

"Joy is right," Liza said. "Friends have to work at getting along. It's the same for husbands and wives. Isn't it, Joy?"

Joy blinked. She opened her mouth,

but no words came out. Eddie knew exactly what had happened. Joy had been tricked into being speechless. Tricked by Liza!

Joy's face turned red. "I need to go and see someone," she finally said. "Liza has reminded me of something very important. I just hope I'm not too late."

"Who do you need to see?" Eddie asked.

"Someone I really love," Joy told the kids. "And it's time I told him so."

Joy hugged each child. "Good-bye!"

"Wait," Liza said, pulling the scarf from around her neck. "Give this to your husband."

"You did it," Howie told Liza after Joy left. "You helped Joy make up with Santa — and Eddie make up with Melody!"

Liza shrugged. "I just hope I wasn't too late. After all, tonight is Christmas Eve."

12

A Package of Proof

Before the kids finished their Doo-dlegum Shakes, the sky darkened. Thick clouds rolled over Bailey City. Giant snowflakes fell and the wind whipped up snowdrifts.

"We better get home," Howie said. "It looks like we're in for another big snowstorm."

"Aren't you worried?" Melody asked Liza. "What if Santa can't find his way in the snow?"

Liza smiled. "I'm not a bit worried. This snowstorm is the perfect cover for Joy to travel in. I bet she's taking off for the North Pole right now!"

"You never proved that Joy is Mrs. Claus," Eddie said. "And I'm not going to believe it unless you wrap up proof and put it under my Christmas tree!"

Liza didn't argue. Instead, she wished her friends a Merry Christmas and went home.

On Christmas Day, Liza wore new mittens and a hat when she met her friends to go sledding.

Fresh snow had turned the city into a winter wonderland, but Eddie didn't scoop up a single snowball. He didn't kick snow at anyone. He didn't even try to put snow down their backs.

Liza put her hand on Eddie's forehead. "Are you sick?" she asked. "Do you have a fever?"

Eddie shook his head.

"Are you still mad?" Melody asked. "I'm really sorry I teased you yesterday."

"No," Eddie said. "I'm not mad."

"Then what is it?" Howie asked. "You're acting like you didn't get a single present for Christmas."

"I got presents," Eddie finally admitted. "In fact, I got exactly what I wanted — a new, improved, super-duper Zirlot Bug Squasher!"

"That's great," Melody said, jumping up and down in the snow. "Your grandmother must have bought it last July."

Eddie shook his head. "My grandmother didn't give it to me. It didn't come from my dad, either."

"Then who gave it to you?" Howie asked.

"Joy," Eddie said.

Howie laughed and slapped Eddie on the back. "It looks like you got that package of proof you wanted after all!"

Liza grinned and pulled a note from her pocket. "I found a surprise under my tree, too." She read the note out loud. "'Thanks for the scarf.'" It was signed S.C.

"Maybe S.C. really is Santa Claus," Howie shouted.

Melody nodded. "And he's Joy's husband. We saved Christmas after all!"

"If Joy is really Mrs. Claus," Eddie said with a laugh, "then I have to say Santa is one lucky man!"

Debbie Dadey and Marcia Thornton Jones have fun writing stories together. When they both worked at an elementary school in Lexington, Kentucky, Debbie was the school librarian and Marcia was a teacher. During their lunch break in the school cafeteria, they came up with the idea of the Bailey School Kids.

Recently Debbie and her family moved to Fort Collins, Colorado. Marcia and her husband still live in Kentucky, where she continues to teach. How do these authors write together? They talk on the phone and use computers and fax machines!

Learn more about Debbie and Marcia at their Web site, www.BaileyKids.com!

**Ready for more spooky fun?
Then here's a sneak peek
at the brand-new series from
best-selling authors,
Marcia Thornton Jones
and Debbie Dadey!**

#1
Ghost Class

Cassidy stumbled over to the wall and flipped on the light switch. She spun around to see a boy about her age, sitting in her desk. He had dark hair that stuck up on top. He wore denim overalls and a striped shirt with a collar. She stared at his tattered shoes until his laughter made her look into his brown eyes.

"How did you do that?" Cassidy asked the boy, but he wouldn't stop laughing. "That wasn't funny at all," she told him.

She stepped toward the desk. "You'd better quit laughing," she warned. She reached over to grab him, but her hand closed around nothing except air — very cold air.

Cassidy's mouth dropped open as she hugged her own dusty arms. She had never felt such a chill. For the first time, Cassidy noticed that the boy wasn't normal. He shimmered around the edges. He was so pale that Cassidy could see right through him. He reminded her of a glowing green-frosted bubble. The boy stood up from the desk and in that instant, he disappeared.

"Where did you go?" Cassidy asked. "Come back here."

The room was still except for a whisper. "I'm warning you. Leave my desk alone."

At first, Cassidy was scared. Had she really seen a ghost? Then Cassidy got mad.

Dust covered every surface of the classroom. Mr. Morton would think she did it. "Come back here and clean up this mess!" Cassidy stomped her foot, sending a little dust cloud into the air above her sneakers. She may as well have been talking to the wind, because the boy didn't reappear.

"This is just great," Cassidy snapped. "Some kids get pen pals — I get a ghost bully."

Suddenly, a noise made Cassidy freeze. Maybe the ghost was back! She whirled around. Jeff and Nina stood at the door to the playground.

"Did you guys see that?" Cassidy asked.

"See what?" Jeff and Nina said together.

"The ghost boy," Cassidy told them.

Jeff laughed. "Yeah, right. I think I just saw a ghost boy skateboarding around the playground."

Nina put her hand on Jeff's shoulder. "I

think she's serious. Cassidy really saw something."

"I'm serious, too." Jeff said with a grin. "Serious about the trouble Cassidy's going to be in when Mr. Morton sees this mess. Maybe the Ghostville ghost can help you blast this mess away," he teased.

Cassidy glared at Jeff as she stomped to the back of the room to grab a mop. "I'm not joking," she said. "I just saw a ghost right here in this very classroom."

Jeff tossed a dust mop to Cassidy. "Next you'll think that mop is a dancing skeleton."

"It's not fair," Cassidy mumbled as she swished the mop across the floor. "Not fair. Not fair. Some ghost made the mess and I have to clean it up. Not fair. Not fair. Not fair."

Cassidy stomped on the mat by the back door extra hard. She was so mad she didn't notice that something weird

"What changed your mind?" Howie asked.

"My dad came home late last night. He's going to stay for Christmas." Eddie smiled broadly. "My dad said it was time we had Christmas joy at our house."

was happening — the little rug underneath her feet was bunching up all on its own. It wiggled, it squirmed, it bubbled, it scrunched. Suddenly, Cassidy teetered. Then she fell down right on the seat of her pants.

From somewhere in the empty basement came the sound of laughter. . . .